ANOMALY

A NHYIRA FILES MYSTERY · NIAPA VALLEY

Theastarr Valerie

EMPRESS ROYALE PUBLISHING

Books By Theastarr Valerie

Nhyira Files Mystery Series

Murder in Zaire Valley
A Fatal Bite

Worth The Wait Series

The Road That Led To Love
Not So Happily Ever After

Novels

Becoming a Royal Princess
True Player For Real

*For a preview of upcoming books, follow TS Valerie
(autrice_tsvalerie) on Instagram.*

Anomaly (Nhyira Files Mystery Book 3)

Empress Royále Publishing
"Everything tells a story..."
1-646-468-3114

Cover photo by iofoto from Adobe Stock

ISBN 9798985358384

Dedication

To God, the Greatest mystery writer from eternity to eternity, thank You.

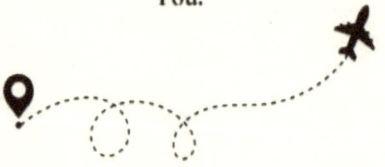

To all the men and women who have devoted their lives to solving mysteries.

To all the Parents, Educators, Members of the Judiciary System, Medical Professionals, Mystery Lovers, Problem Solvers, Researchers, Authors...

This book is for you.

Thank you for all your hard work.

"It is the glory of God to conceal a thing: but the honour of kings is to search out a matter."

Proverbs 25:2 (KJV)

Chapter 1

Glistening sun ✔
Luxury hotel ✔
Infinity pool ✔
Morning swim ✔

Nhyira Enosis celebrated her 25th birthday at the *Saseive Grande Hotel* in *Teedland, Amethyst Island*. She basked in the sun's warmth as she watched it rise over the horizon.

25 signified a quarter of a century. To Nhyira it symbolized over a decade without her parents. Though at times she cried, she knew that death was a part of life; something that many people didn't like to think about.

However, this birthday trip was special because she celebrated it with her loved ones. Her aunt Poet, best friend Mayleigh, and their neighbor Lively. Four women each with a story of overcoming trials; but women who understood the goodness of God.

A mere three years ago, Nhyira didn't want to hear anything about this invisible ruler of the universe, but she gave her heart to HIM after a near death experience last year. It was a decision she didn't regret.

After a week of fun in the sun, Nhyira was ready to get back to reality.

25 is going to be an EXCELLENT year.

"There you are," Mayleigh calls out to Nhyira.

"Were you looking for me?"

"Do you know what time it is?"

"I am enjoying the ambience of this beautiful place."

"It's 7:10. The taxi is coming for us in the next hour and twenty minutes."

Nhyira jumps up from the chaise lounge. "Oh no, I didn't even finish packing."

"Not to worry, your aunty finished it for you. Come on girl." Mayleigh pulls Nhyira. "We gotta go."

"Go back, go back," Lively shrieks.

"What are you freaking out about?"

"Come on Poet, put it back, I want to see the weather."

"I thought something bad happened. Don't scare me like that."

"So-rry," Lively laughs.

Poet throws a pillow at her.

"Turn it up," Lively insists.

> "... Today will be a sweltering 100 degrees; the highest temperature recorded for this season. Hope you have your sunblock. In other news, Canei Zeriolor, an airhostess based here in Amethyst Island has been reported missing for 2 days. Anyone with information please contact the local law enforcement..."

"Such sad news," Poet says, turning off the TV.

"I know. We've heard many reports of young people going missing around the world. But here in Starr Islands, that's unheard of. I hope they find her. Maybe Nhyira should get on the case. She is the **best** crime solver I know."

"She's the only one you know," Poet sneers. "But you are right, my niece is the best."

40 minutes later, Mayleigh brings out a tray of *Sparkling Passion Fruit Cider* and *Powdered Marshmallow Drizzles*. "Toast and a quick snack before our flight."

"I'm ready." Nhyira twirls in her birthday outfit.

Poet whistles. "Now **this** is the look of a 25-year-old. I love your new wardrobe."

Nhyira laughs, knowing that her aunt made a slight quip at her former drab clothing. She went from *plain to popping* in a matter of months. It was a fight to break out of her skinny jeans and tees, but she enjoyed dressing up from time to time. Just in case she wanted to feel comfortable again, she had a secret suitcase full of her comfy clothes.

Mayleigh and Lively nod in agreement.

Nhyira opted to wear an eburnean Grecian dress and gladiator sandals. She finished her outfit with coral dangling earrings and a braided bob.

"Thanks ladies. I'm trying," Nhyira giggles.

"Who's ready to toast?" Mayleigh announces.

Mayleigh lifts her glass. "Here's to year 25."

"CHEERS!" the women sing.

Nhyira sips her cider and exhales elatedly.

Time to go home.

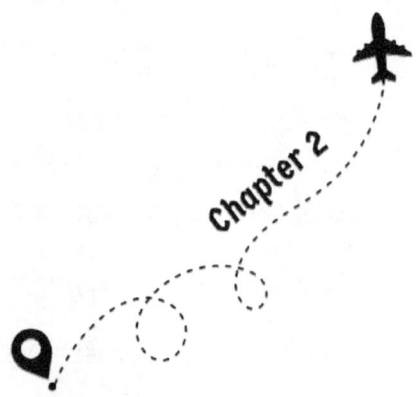

Chapter 2

While they waited for the taxi, a bellhop approaches Nhyira at the gift shop. "Need any help?" the man asks.

"No thank you," Nhyira smiles at him.

"The name's Zeki Montealpi. If you need anything, I'll be right over there," he points to a nearby counter.

"Taxi's here," Mayleigh calls out.

"Let me get that for you." Zeki grabs Nhyira's luggage and places it in the trunk. He then proceeds to assist the other ladies with their luggage.

"Thank you, young man." Lively proceeds to hand him a tip.

"No, no. I'm honored to help you lovely ladies. I hope you enjoyed your stay at the *Saseive Grande*."

"We did," Nhyira nods.

"Where are you from?" Zeki inquires.

"*Njapa*."

He stares at Nhyira. "I didn't catch your name."

"Nhyira."

The man's eyes widen. "*Njapa*? Nhyira? As in **ENOSIS**?"

"I guess you've heard of me?"

Zeki shakes her hand. "It is my pleasure to meet you Nhyira Enosis. You're really popular around here. Probably in the entire Starr Islands. My sister loves your books: **Veisiejai House Murder** and **Food, Sweet Murder**. Can I please get a photo?"

"*SHE'S ENGAGED!*" Mayleigh broadcasts.

"Oh, I'm sorry. I didn't know. Lucky man," Zeki responds, disappointedly.

"Bet you are. Come on Nhyira, taxi's ready to leave." Mayleigh pulls Nhyira into the car.

"It was nice meeting you." Nhyira waves to Zeki innocuously.

"What was that all about?"

Nhyira stares blankly at Mayleigh. "What?"

"Can't you see when a man's flirting with you?"

"Flirting? Oh please. It was innocent. I'm not going to see him again. He was being nice."

"Right! Tell that to your fiancé."

"Akio trusts me," Nhyira counters.

"Nhyira, in case you didn't know, you're a celebrity in Starr Islands. You have to be careful," Mayleigh reiterates.

"Celebrity? I'm an ordinary woman. I don't ascribe to statuses."

"I know you don't, but other people think differently. You can't go around talking to everyone and giving out your personal information like that. Be kind, but *wise* at the same time."

"That's why I have my best friend." Nhyira side hugs Mayleigh. "Aunty, what's on your mind?"

Poet gazes at Nhyira. "Sorry. I was thinking about that missing woman from the news."

"It's bothering you that much?"

"Scary to think about."

Nhyira becomes somber. "Unfortunate situation, but you don't need to live in fear. Justice is always served; if not on earth, in Heaven. Don't you worry. I know how you feel about death and crimes."

"You think it's a crime?" Poet shrieks.

"Maybe you shouldn't watch the news so much. It still makes you anxious," Nhyira replies, referring to her aunt's four decades in prison for a crime she didn't commit.

"We're here," Lively declares, interrupting the conversation.

Chapter 3

Nhyira grabs her bags from *Carousel 358* and tosses them in the cart.

Mayleigh struggles to put her luggage in a cart. "Do you and Akio have any plans for tonight?"

"Yes, he wanted to celebrate my birthday with me."

"You mean he wanted to be the last face you saw before your special day ended?" Poet teases.

"You know Akio; Mr. Sentimental," Nhyira blushes at the thought of her fiancé.

"Can you blame him? The man's loved you since he met you at my diner," Mayleigh reflects.

"I'm happy you two are no longer causing trouble," Lively jokes.

"You won't let us live that down, will you?"

Lively gives a disapproving gesture. "No Nhyira. But I am glad that you two found one another."

The foursome moves further in the line for the scanner. Upon entering every Starr Island, passengers are required to scan their luggage.

"Ma'am, please come with me," a heavily bearded guard barks at Nhyira.

"What's wrong?"

Ignoring her question, the man continues walking to a secluded room, located at the back of the airport.

Nhyira stares at him. "What's happening? Why am I here?"

The man closes the door, leaving Nhyira in anguish.

What's going on? Is it some sort of joke?

Hesiquio Zevallos walks into the interrogation room at the *Njapa Jailhouse*, stunned to see his wife's best friend sitting on the chair.

"Hesiquio, what's happening? No one's said anything to me since I got off the line at the airport. Where are the others?"

"The ladies are fine. I've asked them to stay away until we're done questioning you," he replies.

"Questioning me for what?"

With gloved hands he holds up a gold and silver duffle bag. "Is this yours, Nhyira?"

"Is that a trick question?"

"Just answer the question."

"Yes, it's my bag. I bought it for my trip."

"Can you tell me what's in the bag?"

Nhyira scans Hesiquio's face to see if he was joking. When she realized that he came to her in official officer capacity, she replies, "Um, extra clothes, toiletries, my camera, and a map of *Amethyst Island* for my **travel room** in the mansion."

Hesiquio sits across from Nhyira. "Nhyira, I hate to say this, but you're in serious trouble."

"Why?"

"The items you named aren't in this bag."

"That's impossible. I packed it myself."

"Are you sure you didn't pick up someone else's bag?"

"There were no other bags that color on the carousel. Believe me I looked. That's a limited-edition *Royal McGovern* duffle bag," Nhyira declares. "Only a few were created. Can you tell me what was found in the bag?"

"A razor blade, bloody sweatpants, and $100K."

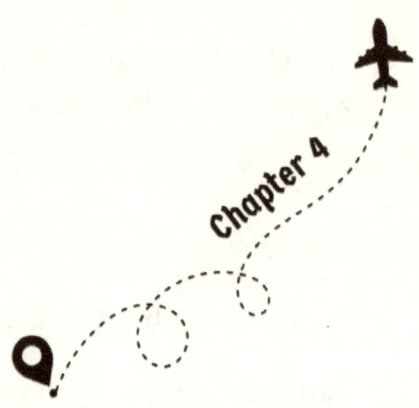

Chapter 4

"**That's** IMPOSSIBLE," Nhyira cries. "I don't carry around that kind of money in my bag."

Hesiquio taps on the desk for emphasis. "Now do you see why you were pulled aside and brought here for questioning?"

"Can I see the bag? This has to be a mistake. I DID NOT pack those things."

Hesiquio pushes the bag to Nhyira. "Don't touch it."

"I want to see inside."

He opens the bag for her.

Nhyira points to a spot above the inner zipper. "There. That's where my initials were engraved. This is NOT my bag."

Officer Zevallos zips the bag. "But you just said it was."

"Now I'm telling you that it's not my bag."

"Nhyira, I trust you, but this doesn't look good for you."

"Call Akio please. I don't want to speak to anyone else."

"You don't want to call your lawyer?"

"AKIO!"

Akio walks over to Officer Zevallos. After being in the jailhouse waiting room for an hour, he was finally able to see his fiancée. His surprise birthday plans were placed on hold when Nhyira's aunt informed him that she was brought in for questioning. He immediately left his home in *Kanomatton* and drove to *Njapa*.

"She's in the interrogation room," Hesiquio says.

Closing the door behind him, Akio kisses Nhyira. "*Mia Bella*, this hurts my heart."

Nhyira begins to cry. "They're saying all these bad things about me, Akio. That's **not** my bag. I don't know where my bag is. Someone took my bag," her voice trails off in muted sobs.

"I'm going to call our lawyer."

"Can we pray first? I'm supposed to be celebrating my 25th birthday with the man I love, yet I'm stuck in jail. What kind of birthday present is this?"

Akio takes her hands and begins to pray.

Olek Pais, Esq. walks into the interrogation room of his latest client, a 25-year-old *Njapa* author; his second case in less than a year.

After passing the bar, he was hired to work on Mayleigh Zevallos' – then known as Mrs. Antao's - murder case. Now a few months later, he was called in by Akio Qvareli to work on his fiancée's case.

Pulling up a chair next to Akio, he looks at his client. "It's weird seeing you on this side. You're *Njapa's Crime Solver*, now you're sitting in jail as a criminal?"

"I didn't do it, Olek," Nhyira cries.

"We'll prove your innocence. First, we have to find out whose blood is on those sweatpants. Then, figure out how the items got in a bag *similar* to yours, all while you were in transit," her lawyer rattles.

"This has to be an inside job," Nhyira states knowingly. "There's no way anyone could pull off a crime like this otherwise."

Olek nods. "I agree with you, but who would do it? What is their motive?"

"I can't do anything from in jail." She looks at Akio. "You're going to have to help me."

Akio grasps her hands. "Of course, *Mia Bella*; anything to get you out of here."

"Olek, can I speak to Akio alone?"

"Sure," he gets up and exits the room.

Akio kisses Nhyira's hair. "I know this isn't the time, but you look beautiful. I love everything."

She blushes, "Thanks *Occhisio*."

"What's the plan?"

"When the blood results from the sweatpants returns, we'll go from there," Nhyira informs.

"I don't want you spending the night here."

"I've been writing crime novels for years. Maybe this will be my best book to date. I get firsthand experience of life behind bars and how the justice system works from this end."

"Only you would think of making a story out of this," Akio exhales.

"Think about it, my first two books were written in third person. This one will be raw and filled with **my emotions**. I know I'm innocent so I'll just look at it as research."

Akio jerks his head in disagreement. "You don't need to research anything from behind bars. This is unnecessary."

The Echo Journal

CRIME SOLVER TURNED MURDERER

February 8, 2001

When travel turns deadly! *The murder weapon of slain 26 year old Canei Zeriolor was discovered in a gold and silver limited edition Royal McGovern duffle bag.*

When news broke out in Amethyst Island on January 28th of the airhostess who'd been missing from work for 2 days, investigators searched and found her body in a hotel closet.

In a horrific twist, the weapon was discovered in the duffle bag of Njapa's Crime Solver, Nhyira Enosis, upon her entrance at Ft. Campaign International Airport, Celgagoas. Along with the murder weapon - a razor blade - airport personnel discovered a bloodied sweatpants, and $100K. The news came as a shock to many citizens of Starr Islands who's been following Nhyira's crime solving feats and reading her bestselling novels.

The Coroner stated that the killer made a small incision in Canei's neck where she bled for some time followed by strangulation with the sweatpants.

Canei's parents have asked that the public allow for a peaceful time of grieving as they deal with the loss of their loving daughter.

No motive has been listed in official police reports.

BY: LEGEND GOLD

Chapter 5

Mayleigh twirls her fork around her *Miomei Pasta* as she sat for dinner with her husband and stepson. "Do you see what they wrote about her in the newspaper? A severe defamation of her character."

Hesiquio taps his son's plate, "Miró, eat your vegetables."

"Chill dad, I'm not a baby. I'm going to be 16 this year."

"Oh Mr. Adult, aye?"

"Can I be excused? Mayleigh looks perturbed. I don't want to get involved in y'all business," he says taking his plate.

Hesiquio nods to his son.

"Are you going to tell me about the investigation?" Mayleigh blurts.

"You know I can't."

"But, I'm your wife. She's my **best friend**."

Hesiquio touches her hand. "While you know I love you very much, it goes against the oath I took as an officer."

"What about the oath we took as husband and wife?"

"Now that's not fair. You know I can't tell you."

Mayleigh begins to laugh. "That's what I get for marrying a *standup guy*; always abiding by the rules. I knew you wouldn't have said anything. Still thought I'd try."

"Oh, you were kidding?" he exhales, relieved.

"Of course. I would never try to undermine your authority. That's one of the reasons I married you. I respect you, Hesiquio." Mayleigh smiles, walking over to sit on his lap. "Now, since you want to speak about oaths, how about you do the dishes."

"Mayleigh!"

"Don't **Mayleigh** me. You vowed to help out in the kitchen, which includes doing the dishes."

Hesiquio picks his wife up and carries her over the dining room threshold. "I'd be honored my lady. When you have a woman who cooks as excellent as you do, I have no problem doing the dishes."

"Such a good man."

He playfully winks at her. "Now, when I'm finished with these dishes we can—"

"HESIQUIO, Miró can hear everything we're saying."

"What?" he shrugs. "I was **going** to say we can watch *Underwater Splash.*"

Mayleigh rolls her eyes, "Oh no, not another documentary."

"You thought I was just a **pretty** face? I'm well informed."

"Alright *Encyclopedia H.*" Mayleigh grins, going up the stairs. "I'll be waiting..."

"I'm coming, I'm coming," Hesiquio whistles.

Chapter 6

Lively rings the bell at the **Veisiejai House**, elated to tell her best friend the news.

Poet runs to open the door. "Why are you ringing down my doorbell?"

"I got it."

"What exactly did you get?"

"The permit to lease my house for short term rental agreements."

Poet pulls Lively inside.

"Not so hard," Lively rubs her arm.

Pouring them cups of *Cobalt Tea*, Poet stares at her friend. "Do you need money? Why the sudden interest in renters?"

"You know I don't need money. What an insult. I thought I'd utilize my house for people who want to stay in *Njapa* in a location with a homey feel. My house is large enough to have guests."

"I get that you want to open up your home to practice being friendly," Poet pauses, "but how do you screen these would be renters?"

"We correspond online."

"O-online? Since when are you down with technology?"

"Did you forget I worked as a Systems Analyst for two decades until the nameless man took over my company?"

"Yes, yes," Poet nods, "you did tell me that."

"My first guest will be here later. Her name's Xieny Fejős; early thirties. She's going to do a short course at *Affair Wedding Studios* in town to complete her Floral Design degree."

"That's a thing? What happened to going to school to become a teacher or obstetrician? Something like that. *Floral Design?* That doesn't even sound feasible in our society."

"You'd be surprised how many floral designers make millions. The most expensive thing on a wedding budget is the flowers."

"Lively, I don't like the idea of you entertaining some stranger in your house."

"It's too late to turn her down now. Besides, she seems nice from online."

"Didn't you read of people who got murdered from online predators?"

"You need help, Poet. Don't be so pessimistic. We're supposed to be trusting God in all things."

"Okay. Fine. But I want to meet this woman when she comes. Probably ask Akio to run a background check on her."

"Does my opinion not matter?"

"I'm taking precautions. Did you have breakfast?" Poet asks, changing the subject.

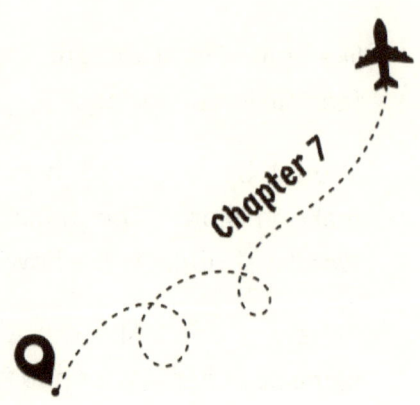

Chapter 7

Kanomatton Underwater Prison

"You're a hard man to track down. It's like you work for the Royal Police Force."

"Yaniv Vénissieux in the flesh. How are you doing mister big shot CEO?"

"What has it been, like 10 years since we graduated? You look the same," Yaniv greets Akio with a brotherly hug.

"You were always the exaggerator. What brings you back home?"

"Is there somewhere we can go to talk, privately?"

"My office," Akio gestures. "Follow me."

Yaniv plops down on the tan couch near the door of Akio's office. "Mr. Big Warden. Good ol' Akio. How are your parents?"

"Oh Mr. and Mrs. World Travelers? I don't even know where they are now. They practically live on the cruise ship."

"Not everyone can afford a 365-day cruise around the world."

"You certainly can," Akio chuckles.

Yaniv Vénissieux was the CEO of Royal Celgagoan Airlines, a business he started at the age of 19. He was considered a pioneer for Starr Islands' younger generation.

"Back to what brings you here."

Yaniv sits up in the seat. "You read the article about the missing woman found dead in her hotel room in *Amethyst Island*?"

Akio nods, "Yeah, what about it?"

"That little article has sent my sales plummeting. I'm afraid that RCA is taking a hard hit because of protesters wanting justice against a Nhyira Enosis, *Njapa's Crime Solver*."

Akio clears his throat. "You haven't heard of her?"

"Since I travel frequently, I don't keep up to date with local news. Canei's entire family is distraught over her death." Yaniv motions to a chair closer to Akio. "Not many people know this, but Canei and I met in *Ft. Campaign* 2 years ago. We dated for a while, but it didn't work out because of my constant travels. She was based in *Amethyst Island* and the distance got too much for her. Her family blamed me for breaking her heart. They didn't like that she stayed on working for me even though we'd broken up."

"I'm sorry for your loss. Did you come to confess..."

"Akio, bro, you think I killed her? NO WAY! We may not have worked out, but I cared for her."

"Then why did you come?"

"I figured you knew something about this crime solver, since she's popular in *Njapa*, which isn't too far from here."

Akio shifts in his seat. "Actually, I know her really well."

Yaniv's eyes widen. "How so?"

"Nhyira's my fiancée."

"Get outta town," Yaniv grins. "You're engaged to a celebrity? This puts me in an awkward situation."

"Why is that?"

"Canei's parents want to petition to have Nhyira's trial date pushed up. They told me if I had any way of helping, they'd forgive me."

"I see. So, this is more about your image than the truth?"

"It's not like that, man."

"Look Yaniv, Nhyira didn't do anything, okay!"

"Calm down. I'm not blaming her. But Canei's parents are pushing hard. They're waiting for me to return with the news that Nhyira will be imprisoned for killing their daughter."

"Stop saying that. Nhyira didn't kill anyone. Don't even put that out in the atmosphere."

"I believe you. I trust your judgment. Keep this between you and me. I don't want my company's name to be dragged further into a scandal. However, if there is any way I can help you or your fiancée, contact me." He hands Akio his business card.

"Thanks. Again, I'm sorry for your loss."

"Sorry your girl's in jail."

Chapter 8

Later that night, Akio brings the newspaper to Nhyira.

Nhyira laughs hysterically.

"What's so funny?"

"They couldn't have thought of a clever title? *Crime Solver Turned Murderer* is the **best** they could come up with?"

"This is not a joke, Nhyira. I don't care what the title is. Your name is in a newspaper for being a murderer. That's funny to you?"

"Come on *Occhisio,* I didn't do anything. Why does it seem like you're more anxious than I am? Lighten up."

Akio huffs furiously. "Will you stop making a joke about this? It's not funny!"

"Would you prefer that I am on the floor crying hysterically so you can hug me and tell me it'll be okay? Well guess what? I already know it's going to be okay. That's why I'm not worried."

"Your aunt spent **forty** years in prison for a crime she didn't commit, in case you forgot."

"Don't do that. I think about that every day. Watching her try to adapt in normal society has been tough, but she's adjusting. The justice system has gotten better since her release and justice will be served in my case. I trust God."

"Some justice system this is."

"The difference between our cases is implicating **evidence.** They found the evidence in my *supposed* luggage and I have nothing to prove my innocence."

"What are we going to do? I can't sleep properly knowing the woman I love is in jail for something she didn't do."

Nhyira stares at Akio. "What if you find out that I'm guilty, would you still be this willing to help?"

"You're still making jokes."

"I don't know what you want from me," she kisses his cheek. "I'm fine. No one's treating me bad in here."

"But your name's tarnished in society."

"AND? Jesus was innocent, yet they still killed HIM. HIS name was tarnished, yet it is the **only** name by which demons flee."

"What are you trying to say?"

"God turns our trials into triumph. Trials are a part of the journey. If Christ wasn't publicly humiliated and died for our sins, then mankind wouldn't have the greatest example of sacrifice and love. Before the foundation of the Earth, God knew this would happen to me. And if HE sees that it should be a part of my journey, then so be it."

Akio stares at her in amazement. "When did you become this deep in the Word?"

"I have a good teacher," she winks.

"Thanks for reminding me where to focus."

"We're a tag team and I love you."

"I love you more."

He reflects on the day they met, thankful that their paths crossed.

"Can you help me?"

"You know I will," Akio reassures.

"I need you to get my case files notebook and bring it to me. I want to start writing down clues so that we can work with Mr. Pais to get me out of here. Aunty Poet knows where it is."

Chapter 9

Lively drops the kitchen towel on the counter and trots to the door. Her house guest was here.

Opening the door, she smiles at the woman. "Welcome to *Njapa*. Come in."

Xieny scans the main room, drops her bag and hugs Lively.

"Oh. You're a hugger," Lively flinches.

"I am. Thank you for welcoming me into your home. It's hard to find a decent place on my student salary."

"Would you like something to drink?"

"Some water would be fine."

Lively hands her a glass of water. "Did you find the house okay?"

"There are only two houses in the area."

"Tell me about yourself." Lively leads the woman to a chair.

"My name's Xieny Fejős as you know. 34 years old. I have a degree in Event Planning, but needed this certificate in Floral Design to help with the business I want to own one day."

"When does your course start?"

"It's a 3-week course. It has already started. I'm playing catch up. Apparently, I mixed up the dates; thought it was starting next week." Xieny sips her water.

"Let me show you to your quarters. I hope it's to your liking. I don't have much modern amenities that you young people like, but there is internet."

"Oh, that's alright. I'll be spending most of my time studying."

Lively leads Xieny to a room. "This is it."

"Wow, it's gorgeous," Xieny beams. "I like the view of the garden."

"If you need anything else you can ask. I want your stay here to be pleasant."

"Thanks. I think I'm gonna shower and head to bed. I'm tired."

"Good night," Lively waves, closing the door behind her.

Detective
Notes

Property of Nhyira Enosis

NHYIRA ENOSIS

DETECTIVE

CRIME

Airhostess found dead in Saseive Grande Hotel.

SUSPECTED MURDERER

ME (WHATTTTTTTT??)

DECEASED

Canei Zeriolor

CONNECTION TO THE DECEASED

None

LOCATION OF MURDER

Saseive Grande Hotel

WEAPONS

Razor blade and sweatpants

MY NOTES

I WAS FRAMED!! My limited edition Royal McGovern duffle bag was replaced with someone else's. The pseudo bag contains a razor blade, bloodied sweatpants and $100K.

Possible suspects and motive: ????
I don't know. None of this makes sense.

Motive: NO CLUE!!

FOLLOW UP

I don't even know where to begin. I need more information. I'm truly stumped.

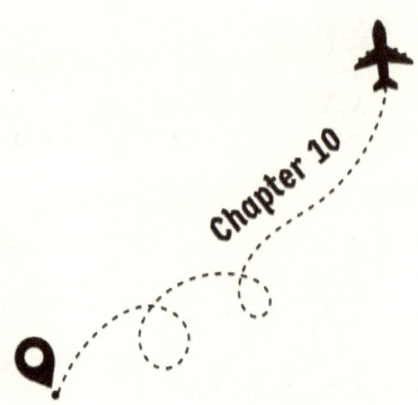

Chapter 10

Xieny walks into the grand kitchen; surprised to see Lively up and at the breakfast table.

"Oh good, you're up. I saw how tired you were last night and didn't want to wake you. I know students need as much sleep as they can get."

"Morning," Xieny yawns. "What smells so good?"

"I didn't know what you eat. You can leave back what you don't want."

"I'm hungry. I would never refuse food. Thanks for cooking."

Excited to have her first house guest in decades, Lively cooked *Ifeto Waffles* and *Blossomed Eggs*. She also added *Medallion Cereal* and *Lavender Milk* in case Xieny wanted something crunchy.

"Got any plans before your class?"

"I thought maybe I'd take a jog around the park," Xieny informs.

"You're one of those."

"*Those* what?"

"Health buffs."

Xieny grins. "I **try**. But, running helps me clear my head."

"You need to meet my best friend then. She **loves** to run. She runs with her niece all the time, but her niece isn't here at the moment."

"Where does your friend live?"

"In the mansion across the street."

"I was meaning to ask, is that **The Veisiejai House**?"

"You heard of it?"

"I read about it in a pamphlet at the *Njapa Visitor's Center*."

"What's that face about?"

"Honestly, I love your house, but I was wondering if this town is safe."

"*Njapa's* as safe as it comes," Lively reassures.

"How could you say that with two murders in such close proximity to your home? One in the house next door and the other at the diner."

"I miss the days when things were quiet. I can assure you that *Njapa* is safe. Plus, we have a *Crime Solver.*"

"Police Chief?"

"No, **The Crime Solver**; Nhyira Enosis. She owns the mansion next door."

"Your friend's niece?"

"I'm surprised you haven't heard about her."

"I thought she was a myth of sorts representing many residents in *Njapa*," Xieny quips.

"No myth here. She's real and an excellent crime solver."

"Where is she now?"

"She's around," Lively pauses. She didn't want to divulge too much information about her best friend's niece to the stranger.

"It looks like I've hit a nerve. I'm sorry."

"That's okay. As soon as you're finished, I'll introduce you to my friend, if you're not busy before your run."

"I'd love that."

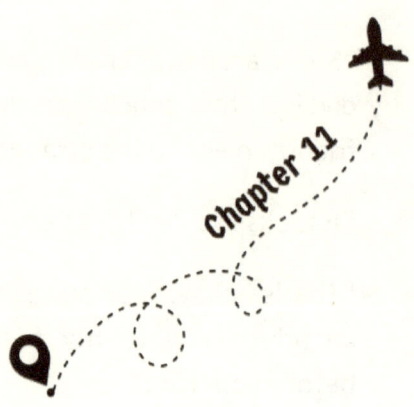

Chapter 11

The clock in the foyer chimed **7AM** when Poet heard the doorbell ring. Although she wasn't expecting anyone, she opened the door.

"Good morning, Poet."

"Hi Lively, I didn't know we had plans today."

"We don't. I want to introduce you to someone."

Poet escorts the ladies into the living room. "Drinks?"

Lively waves her off. "We had breakfast."

Poet glances at Xieny. "And who is this young lady?"

"Poet meet Xieny Fejős, the student I was telling you about."

"Which— Oh, of course." Poet extends her hand. "Nice to meet you, Xieny. Welcome to our town."

"Thank you, ma'am."

"You can call me Poet. Ma'am sounds a little too **old** for me. Yes, I know I'm old," she chuckles. "Floral Design huh? What got you into that career?"

"My degree is in Event Planning, but I'm doing this course to help my business."

"What's the name of your business?"

"I haven't exactly started yet. Finances are tight, but I'm determined to succeed," Xieny shares.

"That's the right attitude. You sound like my niece."

"The *Crime Solver*?"

"You've heard of her?"

"Ms. Lively gave me the rundown."

"She did, did she?" Poet shoots Lively a look.

"Don't worry, she's quite secretive. Whatever secret you have, she hasn't told me."

Poet exhales a sigh of relief. "Have you gotten a chance to see our town?"

"I don't think I'll be doing much sightseeing. Between studying and classes, I'll be resting."

"All work and no play? That's not good for a woman your age. You need to have fun. At least go to **Mayleigh's Diner.**"

Xieny scratches her head nervously. "I-I'm not sure about that one."

"I know you probably heard about a horrible murder there, but don't worry, the murderer is behind bars. Serves him right. He tried to kill my niece," Poet goes off on a tangent.

Lively signals for her to stop.

"I'm sorry. I didn't mean to offload on you like that," Poet apologizes.

"It's okay," Xieny chuckles. "Ms. Lively, I think I'll go for that run now."

Lively puts her hand on her friend's shoulder. "I know this is hard, but you can't share your business with strangers like that. We'll get through it. Nhyira will be released."

"You don't understand, you've never been in jail. First me, then Mayleigh, now my Nhyira? I feel like this is all my fault. I don't want you to be next," Poet sighs.

"How is this your fault?"

"I think I brought a bad omen into *Njapa*."

"That's absurd," Lively scoffs. "None of this is your fault. I'm sorry you spent all those years in prison, but *pleaseeeeeeee* be at peace."

"I don't want anything to happen to anyone. Maybe I should've stayed in *Kanomatton*."

"Now you really need to stop talking. You received your freedom, be thankful. Look forward, not backward."

"It's hard, Lively. I've been out for over 2 years, but my mind is still in prison."

That's why we'll continue to pray for your healing. There's nothing that Jesus can't help us overcome. And **the mind** is something that HE specializes in. You'll get your healing, Poet."

Chapter 12

"**What** are you doing here? Don't you have work?" Nhyira asks her fiancé later that morning.

"I took the day off," Akio reveals. "I can't function at work, knowing you're here."

"It's only been a few days."

"What is Mr. Pais doing to help?"

"He's at the hotel conducting an investigation."

"Aka you're keeping him busy while you solve the case?"

"Yup, pretty much. But, he's happy to assist me."

"Why are you doing this to him?" Akio chortles.

"He said he likes being in my books and would do anything to be a character in my upcoming novel."

"I want him to do his job, Nhyira."

"He is. The information he brings me from the hotel will help me solve the case."

"You're too much."

"That's why you love me."

"I do. I definitely love you," he replies, kissing her.

"That sounds like the lyrics from one of the songs I listened to as a child."

"From *The Miseno Brothers?*"

"Noooo. I know **all** the songs from my favorite band. It was a joke, *Occhisio.*"

"Let's get back to the matter at hand."

"I know you're a warden and all, but lighten up," Nhyira quips. "We're only young once. I want us to have fun no matter what."

He gives her a stern look. "What's next on the agenda?"

"Wow, you just disregarded my speech."

"No *Mia Bella,* but I want you to get out of here."

"You just want your trophy fiancée around for all those fancy dinners."

"Nhyira!"

"Okay, okay, I'll stop." She holds her stomach from the intense giggling.

Nhyira writes on a piece of paper and hands it to Akio.

"What's this?" he asks.

"The next step."

"What do you want me to do?"

"Your friend Yaniv, the one who owns RCA, I need you to get this information from him." She points to the note.

Akio reads the instructions aloud.

NHYIRA ENOSIS

DETECTIVE

MY NOTES

1. Get a list of all the passengers and crew from my flight.

2. Do an intensive background check on everyone; including name changes and/or aliases.

3. Get the names and whereabouts of _every_ airline worker in Amethyst Island and Celgagoas up to a week before the murder.

4. Find out from the Royal McGovern office if anyone purchased one of their limited edition duffle bags during the week I stayed at the hotel. Also find out if anyone sells knockoff bags in Teedland. _I believe the person was monitoring me and purchased the bag to carry out their crime._

Akio inserts the paper in his pocket. "Is that all?"

"For now. That should take a few days. If you need to go to Amethyst Island for any reason, let me know. I'll pay for your airline tickets."

"I'm not taking any money from you. If I need to go, I'll pay for myself. You're my woman and I'll do anything for you. I don't want you worrying about taking care of me financially. There'll be so many other ways you can take care of me after we're married."

Nhyira's face reddens, "If you don't get your mind out of the gutter, Mr. Qvareli."

"That won't be classified as gutter worthy, but something beautiful between a **married** couple."

"I can't with you right now."

"I know; that's why I said *after* we're married," he winks.

Nhyira covers her rosy face.

I love my Occhisio. Always making me blush...

Chapter 13

After stopping for lunch, Akio dials Yaniv's number.

"What's up?" Yaniv greets.

"Did you receive the fax I sent to your office?"

Silence is heard on the other end.

"I got it," Yaniv says, moments later.

"Nhyira asked me to get that information. I figured that you'd have access to most of it."

"I'm getting to help in an official **Nhyira Files** case?"

"What is it with people and my fiancée?"

"Can you ask her to put me in her next book?"

"Yes, I'll ask."

"Thanks man. Do you need help with anything else?"

"Tickets for me and a few officers to go to *Amethyst Island* to question some locals," Akio rattles off.

"Sure man. I'll even give you first-class tickets."

"Economy is fine."

"Nah, no friend of mine will be flying economy. You and your team will get the VIP treatment. If ever you need anything else, let me know," Yaniv replies. "I'll be sure to get the information you asked for, ASAP."

"What about Canei's family? How'd your talk with them go?"

"I haven't spoken to them yet. I'll speak to them at the funeral in a few days."

"Give them my condolences."

"Will do. Stay positive," Yaniv encourages. "Your girl will get out soon."

"Thanks. Later." Akio clicks off the phone and gets to work.

Chapter 14

"**Hey** sweetie." Mayleigh hugs Nhyira. "Sorry I'm late."

"With the hours you work, I'm surprised you could visit at all. I appreciate it."

"After all you've done for me; I'd shutdown that diner if I have to."

"How's the family? I still can't believe you're a stepmother. How's your stepson?"

"Miró's a... *teenage boy* is all I can say."

"That says a lot," Nhyira giggles. "Does he respect you as a mother figure?"

"He's a joy to have. I didn't get the chance to have children of my own before, but that'll soon change."

"What are you saying?"

Mayleigh rubs her stomach. "I'm pregnant."

Nhyira shrieks excitedly.

"Owwww." Mayleigh covers her ears.

"My bad. Why didn't you tell me this before?"

"I only found out this morning."

"Does Hesiquio know?"

"Nah, I didn't wanna tell him until we're in a quiet environment."

"Let me know how he reacts. I'm over the moon at this news. I'm going to be an aunty. How far along are you?"

"9 weeks."

"Mr. Officer wasn't playing any games."

"NHYIRA!"

"What? You know I tell it like it is. Miró's going to be a big brother."

"That should be interesting," Mayleigh quips.

"Not as interesting as Hesiquio fathering a newborn in his old age."

"HEY, watch it. Hesiquio and I are the same age."

"But, you're my best friend," Nhyira giggles. "You're not old to me."

"You're a trip, you know that."

"Do you want a girl or boy?"

"No preference," Mayleigh shrugs. "I'm thankful that I get to experience the joy of motherhood. I never thought I'd get to have children," she wipes tears from her eyes.

"God's timing is definitely not ours."

"You're right. Now I'll be blessed with two children."

"I celebrate with you," Nhyira beams.

"Now that I've shared my news, let's talk about what's happening with you."

"Well, I'm still in jail, as you can see."

"I meant how are you emotionally? I know what it feels like to be behind bars. This was me a few months ago."

"To be honest, only Akio and Aunty Poet are up in arms about this. I'm calm."

"I understand that too. I wish you didn't have to go through this ordeal. It's not a nice feeling being known as the woman that *was in jail*."

"There could be worse titles."

"You're correct. With all that you've been through since moving to *Njapa*, I know that you have a powerful ministry ahead."

"I'm still wrapping my head around the concept of God turning a bad situation into good. I know we use the term *trial into triumph*, but I still don't fully understand what it means," Nhyira admits.

"You will get your clarity. When I was in here, I didn't know what the purpose was until after my release. I met Hesiquio because of it. It may not be a romantic story in the traditional sense, but it's our story. And I wouldn't have it any other way."

"Persecution is **awful**, but the long-term eternal benefit is unexplainable," Nhyira replies, thinking back to the stories she read about the apostles in the Bible.

Chapter 15

Hours later, Nhyira wakes up to see strange eyes staring at her. "Hello, I'm here."

Nhyira gazes at the man, dizzily. "Zeki?"

"Happy to see me?"

"What are you doing in *Njapa*?"

"I took a sabbatical from work to visit you."

Walking to the jail bars she sticks her hand out. "You know I'm engaged right?"

"Yes, yes, I know. Kinda bummed about it, but I thought I'd still visit," Zeki shrugs.

"Why?"

"When I saw **you** were arrested, I couldn't fathom it. I decided to hear from your mouth about what happened."

"Why?" she repeats.

"You're **The Unscrambler**. I know you're innocent, but I'm fascinated by your case."

"You think I'm innocent?"

"Of course, you are. You couldn't even tell I was flirting with you at the hotel. If your friend didn't say you were engaged, I'd have asked for your number."

"Your presence makes no sense to me, but I don't have the strength right now. I hope you enjoy your stay in our town."

"When my sister heard I was coming she begged me to get your autograph. Do you think I can?" He pulls one of her novels out of a bag.

"You have a pen?"

Zeki excitedly hands her a pen. "Thank you so much Nhyira. I know this is weird, but you've made me a happy man."

"It's just an autograph."

"Not 'just', it's **your** autograph. This'll be worth a fortune someday. It's not about the money, but I'll be able to tell people I have an actual *Nhyira Enosis* signature, not some stamped one."

"Okay then."

He opens a pack of chips from the bag and stretches it through the bars. "Want some?"

"No thanks. I'm fine."

"Suit yourself." He retreats his hand.

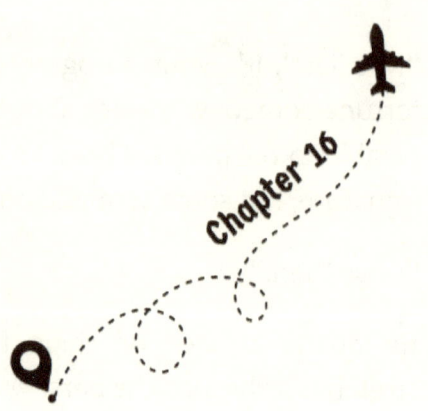

Chapter 16

"**Morning** Hesiquio, is she up?"

"Yeah, she's in writing mode."

Akio motions to the man sleeping in front of the hallway to Nhyira's cell. "Who's that?"

"His name's Zeki; said he met Nhyira during her birthday vacation."

"What is he doing here?" Akio grits.

"Visiting, I guess. He's been here for 2 days."

"I don't like this one bit. Why didn't you call me? Who is this man?"

"Nhyira hasn't complained about him. He isn't causing trouble at the station, either. What's the problem?"

"What about the bro code?"

"She's a grown woman, Akio. If she doesn't see an issue with him, why should I?"

"Would you feel so nonchalant if another man is around your wife for no apparent reason?"

"I trust Mayleigh; she can speak to whoever she wants."

"Well, I'm not that trusting of others around Nhyira. She almost died last year."

"I know that you're worried about her safety, but no one can hurt her here."

"*Right.* Because **nothing** has ever happened in jail before."

"Have you ever heard of any incidents in a Celgagoan jail?"

"Well, no," Akio defends, "but it happens around the world."

"Let's focus on our country. Besides, you should be having this conversation with her. I have work to do." Hesiquio ambles off.

"*Occhisio* you're back," Nhyira screams excitedly until she sees Akio's facial expression. "What's wrong?"

"Who is that sleeping outside the hallway to your cell?"

Nhyira looks around the area. "How am I supposed to know?"

"Don't play games with me. Who is this man who's been visiting you for a few days?"

"It's nothing," she brushes him off.

"What is he doing **here**?" Akio asks.

"He came to town for a vacation and wanted an autograph for his sister."

"How clever of him. I bet he doesn't even have a sister."

"Is this going somewhere?"

"Are you disregarding my feelings?"

66

"I don't *have time* for this, Akio. We should be discussing my case. That's what's important, not Zeki."

"Y'all on a first name basis now? So, you do know him?"

Nhyira rolls her eyes and sits on her bed. "Let me know when you're ready to have a logical conversation. Zeki being here is completely **irrelevant**. You're acting as if you caught him inside the cell with me."

"Why would you put that idea in my head?"

"I'm **NOT** doing this with you! I'm NOT!" she retorts irately. "I can't keep defending myself. I'm *not* her. It's not fair."

"Nhyira, this looks suspicious. I don't want anything to happen to you."

"This isn't about your concern for my safety and you know that. It's about you not trusting me."

"I do trust you. It's *him* that I don't trust."

"If you trusted me, we wouldn't be having this argument right now. GET OUT!"

"You're kicking me out?"

"I don't want to talk to you when you're being irrational and inconsiderate," Nhyira replies. "Mr. Pais can help me with the investigation from now on. I don't want your assistance. I need to focus my energy on solving this case."

"You're serious?" Akio asks.

"Does it look like I'm laughing? GET OUT!"

Chapter 17

After Akio left, Mr. Pais enters her cell.

"What information did you get from the hotel?" she asks, looking at the papers in his hands, ignoring the anger boiling inside.

The nerve of Akio...

Olek hands Nhyira photos and notes he gathered from the hotel. "There weren't many witnesses."

"I figured as much."

"What are you thinking?"

"This has to be an inside job, Olek. Whoever did this crime is no amateur. They thought of everything."

"I wrote that in my notes. The suspect has been to the hotel before. They know the ins and outs; including the location of the surveillance equipment. And they timed the movement of the cameras."

Nhyira stares at the photos. "That hotel is big. Did you check to see if there are doors in between the rooms? Who was in the room next door to Canei?"

"I checked for all of that, but there was no one listed as a guest for any of the adjacent rooms."

"The suspect seems too smart to be captured on camera. I'm ruling out that they climbed through a window. They had to have been in the hotel already and slipped out undetected."

"I found something else." Olek hands the stack of papers to Nhyira.

"What is it?"

"Open it."

Nhyira glances at the articles. "These are all the articles written about me solving crimes. My name is underlined in red in all of the articles. Where'd you find them?"

"I found them in the hotel basement's garbage disposal."

"You know what this means?"

"That you were a deliberate target."

Nhyira nods.

"Unfortunately," Olek adds, "no DNA was found on the papers."

"This is good, Olek. I will add this to my files."

"But there is no DNA evidence."

"I don't deal with the sciences. I deal with words and facts."

"It's fascinating to watch you work. You'd be a great asset to my team. Are you sure you don't want to get into law?" Olek pleads.

"My answer's still **no**."

"That's too bad. What's our next step?"

"Let me go over the notes I have. When you come tomorrow, I'll have an answer for you."

"Nhyira, it's a pleasure working with you." Olek shakes her hand. "See you tomorrow."

Down on her knees, Nhyira begins to pray.

*"Dear God, I come to You in the name of Jesus thanking You for another day. Father, I've been in this cell for one week, but it feels like years. I know I put on a façade in front of others, but You know my deepest thoughts. I cannot hide anything from You. This case is beyond me. It is **about** me and I'm scared. I need the help of the greatest lawyer known: Jesus Christ. Please lead me and all the investigators to the right clues. I pray that my testimony will be great as a result of this horrible ordeal. In Jesus' name I pray, Amen."*

Chapter 18

Mayleigh storms toward Zeki. "I can't believe that you're still here."

"I was on my way to your diner. I wanted to surprise Nhyira with some food."

"What are you still doing here?"

"My flight doesn't leave until in the morning," Zeki replies.

"Have you been sleeping here?"

"I sleep at the hotel."

"I will have you arrested if you don't leave," Mayleigh snaps.

"I'm in a jailhouse ma'am. If I did something wrong, they'd have arrested me already."

"Did you just **MA'AM** me?" Mayleigh scoffs.

"I respect my elders. You're older than me."

"HMPH!"

"There is no reason for me to be arrested," Zeki replies. "I haven't disturbed anyone. Officer Zevallos has been extra kind to me."

"Officer Zevallos, huh?"

"Do you know him?" Zeki asks.

"I'm Mrs. Zevallos."

"Oh," Zeki replies. "Awkward."

"Listen here boy—"

"I'm a man, ma'am."

"Stop that."

"Stop calling me **boy**."

"As I was saying," Mayleigh continues, "you need to leave. You have no business here. Nhyira doesn't need any more friends. Plus, your motives aren't pure. I know you like her."

"She's my friend."

"You're no friend of hers. In fact, the more you stay here the more suspicious you look."

"Why would I be here if I committed a crime?" Zeki counters.

"I don't know; to gloat maybe."

"You're not making any sense."

"Neither is your presence here, Zeki. Go home and move on with your life. Stop pining over a woman who's taken."

"You can't tell me what to do. After I go see her, I'll be on my way."

Chapter 19

"**Hey** girl," Nhyira welcomes.

Mayleigh ignores her greeting. "Why's Zeki still here?"

"Uggh! Not you too."

"Isn't it strange that his vacation location happens to be where you *live*?"

"What do you people want from me? Why are you ganging up on me?"

"We're not ganging up on you," Mayleigh says.

"I know Akio's like a son to you, so he does **nothing** wrong in your eyes, but he was out of line," Nhyira snaps.

"He's wrong for being concerned about you?"

"That's jealousy, not concern. I haven't done anything. He's supposed to trust me."

"You're supposed to take his feelings into consideration as well. You two don't live in the same state and he almost lost you last year."

"But, I'm still here. Why don't we focus on that?"

"I do **not** trust Zeki. Something's not adding up with him."

"Are you a detective now?"

"You're not getting any **red flags** from him? How do you explain his presence here?"

"Zeki's absolutely harmless," Nhyira answers coolly.

"That's not an explanation."

"Mayleigh are you here to add to my annoyance? I already have someone on my list."

"Both your fiancé and I care about you."

Nhyira kisses her teeth.

"That was uncalled for."

"So is this conversation."

"Why aren't you listening to reason?" Mayleigh snaps.

"You're fighting the wrong enemy. This isn't about Zeki. He's not on my suspect list. Most of our conversations surround my books. He likes them."

"He likes **you** not your books. No man visits a woman in jail because he likes her **books**."

Shrugging her shoulders, Nhyira stands akimbo. "Hate to burst your bubble, but I literally don't care about your thoughts on this. I just want to get out of jail."

"You don't **care**?"

"Not when you're spewing folly," Nhyira argues.

"You're insulting me?"

"STOP MAYLEIGH! STOP! I have too much on my mind right now. Everyone's caught up in their own feelings, no one cares about mine. I trust Zeki. If you don't trust me to make the right choices, then you can leave. I don't need this in my life. I need to focus on my case NOT ARGUING." She storms off and plops on her bed.

Chapter 20

A week had passed since her niece was arrested and today was the first time Poet entered the jailhouse. As per Nhyira's request, she wasn't to enter the jailhouse or anything related to criminals. However, Poet could no longer deal with the news about her niece's atrocious behavior.

"I thought I asked that you not come in here?" Nhyira sighs.

"Good night to you too. I haven't seen or heard from you since you left the airport."

"Aunty, I don't want you in here."

Poet sits on the chair in the visitors' area. "I didn't come here to go back and forth with you."

"Please go home."

"Sit down!"

The guard stares at the two women, but he remains silent when he saw the austerity in Poet's expression.

"S-she has t-ten minutes ma'am. Visiting hours has ended," the guard stutters.

"No problem young man. That's more than enough time." Poet faces Nhyira.

Holding her head in her hands, Nhyira tries to zone out the scolding she knew was coming from her aunt. Even though she was 25 years old, her aunt was old school, so she quietly listened.

"Why am I hearing that you asked both Akio and Mayleigh to leave?"

"B-because, t-they were bothe—"

"Speak properly. You had all that mouth to tell them off. Tell me off."

"Aunty, I wouldn't do that to you."

"I may not have known you long, but I KNOW this isn't how your parents taught you to treat others.

Akio is your fiancé. If you can't respect him now then you won't respect him when you are married. And even though Mayleigh is your **best friend**, she is STILL older than you. The respect you give me, you have to give to her as well. Come off whatever high horse you're on because I won't have it. Do you understand me?"

Feeling like a little girl again, Nhyira nods in humiliation. Even though it had been years since she got a '*talking to*' by her parents, her aunt was right. Respect was to be given no matter a person's age.

"Now is not the time to isolate yourself from those who love you," Poet continues. "Zeki is a distraction. I don't care if you're one of those **modern women**. If your man says he doesn't feel comfortable with another man in your company, tell that **other** man to hit the road. Don't let an outsider mess up your relationship with your significant other. If the tables were turned, I'm sure you'd want Akio to get rid of **any** woman who you think is getting his attention. Don't make the same mistake I did with the mayor all those years ago—" Poet stops as she reflects on losing her husband.

Nhyira touches Poet's hand. "I hear you Aunty. I get it. I will apologize. Please don't cry."

Wiping her eyes, Poet exhales. "I'm fine. I just don't want you to ruin it. Relationships are about give and take. You may not have done anything wrong in your eyes, but don't disregard Akio's feelings."

"Thank you for your stern warning," Nhyira replies. "I appreciate it."

Chapter 21

After class ended, Xieny's stomach churned. From the traffic light, she noticed a sign highlighting **Mayleigh's Diner**. She decided to give the restaurant a try since it was highly recommended by the locals.

"Night miss. How may I help you?" Mayleigh hands Xieny a menu.

"I'm starved. Any suggestions?"

"My *Plumberry Pancakes* of course."

"You mean the same pancakes that killed the critic last year? No thanks," Xieny snarls.

"That was an unfortunate event that I didn't cause," Mayleigh replies softly.

"I think I'll try something else. No need for deadly pancakes. I don't want my last meal to be tonight," Xieny jibes.

"I'll see what I can get you," Mayleigh sighs.

"Why the glum look, my love?" Hesiquio probes.

"When will this stigma be lifted from me? I didn't kill the food critic, yet people still look at me like a criminal."

"No need to worry about what others think."

"Easy for you to say, no one looks at you like you'll poison them."

"Haven't you gotten many diner patrons since your release? People love your food. Your diner's packed every day. Everyone's entitled to their opinions, but don't let it get to you."

"I want things to go back to the way it was before all this happened."

"Then you wouldn't have met me." Hesiquio places his chin on his palms.

Mayleigh blushes.

"Xieny's probably like Nhyira; a mystery enthusiast and doesn't mean anything by it."

"You're right. What do you want to take home for Miró to eat?"

"It'll just be me and you tonight. I'll wait until you close the diner."

"What do you mean? Where is he?" Mayleigh inquires.

"He left for the Robotics Tournament in Estonia, today. Did you forget?"

"Estonia?"

"Clearly you weren't paying attention to his presentation last month: *Why Miró Should Go To Estonia.*"

"You know I zone out all those documentaries and smarty pants jargon."

"Then maybe you should begin paying attention. Our son will be into this too," he points to her stomach.

"How do you know it's a boy?"

"I just do."

"You want it to be."

"I know the baby's a boy. I've already been thinking of names."

"Whoaaaa slow down. We still have months to go before the baby arrives," Mayleigh giggles.

"If it's anything I learned from the last time, you can't prepare enough for a baby's arrival. They come whenever they want."

"I can't believe that I'm a mother..."

Chapter 22

Akio exhales as he walks down the hall to Nhyira's cell. He'd been up all night thinking of ways to apologize to her for his insecurity. His night was filled with prayer. Only God knew how to get through to HIS daughter, so Akio trusted HIM to fix the situation. Arguing with his fiancée made him feel sick. Of course, she was right; he had lashed out at her because of his past experience. His ex had left him for one of her clients; a criminal whose case she worked on. It was a devastating experience that he wouldn't wish on anyone.

Nhyira's body ached from all the tossing and turning she'd done the previous night. She massaged her scapula as she grimaced in pain.

She thought all night about what her aunt said... Not allowing outsiders to mess up your relationship; whether from the past or present.

Being in jail didn't leave room for sprucing up, but she tried to make herself look presentable in case Akio visited.

After 10 minutes of pacing the halls, Akio finally mustered the courage to approach Nhyira's cell.

"*Mia Bella*, good morning."

"*Occhisio*," Nhyira cries out.

"I'm sorry," they say in unison.

"Can we speak in the visitor's area?" he asks the guard.

"Only if Ms. Nhyira wants to," the man retorts.

Nhyira nods her head.

Sitting in the visitor's area, Akio clutches Nhyira's hands and stares into her eyes. "I missed you."

"I-I missed you too, Akio. I've been miserable knowing that we weren't speaking. I'm sorry that I yelled at you."

"I'm sorry that I let my emotions get the best of me and I didn't trust you."

"Do you forgive me?"

"Yes. Do you forgive me?"

"I forgive you." She wipes the tears from her eyes.

"Can we please speak about something exciting? I feel as if our conversations surround doom and gloom."

"Let's talk about our upcoming nuptials. Will your parents be in attendance?"

Akio laughs. "They'll be in the front with the world's largest video camera. It's not every day their only child will get married."

"I will be happy to finally meet them in person. Phone calls are impersonal."

"They're excited to meet you too. Have you decided on the date? We have to start marriage counseling."

"Once as I am out of here, we can discuss further details." Nhyira pauses, "What if I never leave?"

"Positive thinking only. You'll be out of here before the month is over."

"Don't speak like that. I don't need my hopes up."

"Our Father is in full control and our hope is in HIM. So yes, get your hopes up. Your hope isn't based on your current situation or feelings. We're going to pray and watch God work."

"You're such a great leader, Akio. I love you."

"I'm thankful to God every day for gifting me HIS daughter. I plan to take very good care of you with HIS leading."

Chapter 23

"**Breaking** News:

'We're live with the mother of slain airhostess, Canei Zeriolor. Mrs. Zeriolor?'

'I hope Nhyira Enosis ROTS in prison for killing my daughter. No bail. No shortened sentence. We're calling for a lifetime in prison or that Starr Islands revoke their *no death sentence* rule. A daughter for a daughter. Make AN EXAMPLE of that wretched girl from *Njapa*! You WILL PAY!'

'Thank you, Mrs. Zeriolor—'"

Poet shuts off the TV and throws her glass across the room. "WHYYYYYYYY?"

Lively runs over and holds her best friend's hands. "Control yourself."

"Get off of me," she retorts angrily. "Look at how they're dragging Nhyira through the mud. **Death sentence**? What is wrong with that woman? I can't lose my only family member. I don't have anyone else," Poet continues softly.

"You can't lash out like this. It's not going to change anything. We're supposed to be praying. The last thing I want is for you to hurt yourself on top of your niece's imprisonment."

"They're lying. She didn't do it."

"We know that," Lively nods. "Everything will come to light. Trust God, Poet, trust God."

"HE'd better get my niece out of that jail cell. Prison is an ugly place."

"Breathe. Just breathe. That's it, that's it. Let's go over to my house. I'll cook us lunch."

Chapter 24

"There you are," Xieny greets when Lively opens her front door.

Lively observes a well laid out dining room table. "What's all this?"

"I made lunch. It's my way of showing appreciation for all you've done for me, Ms. Lively."

"Xieny, you didn't have to cook. You're my guest. Meals are part of your living arrangements."

"I only wanted to show my appreciation."

"Thank you. I am grateful. What did you make?"

"Whipped Coriander Flatbread and Breaded Hazelnut Pork. For dessert I made Grapeseed Ice-Cream; your favorite," Xieny announces.

At the mention of Grapeseed, Lively's eyes glisten with joy.

"Where are you going?" she asks Xieny.

"I am heading to class early today. I want to go over my speech for the presentation."

"I can't believe how fast the time went by." Lively grabs a spoon to eat her ice-cream.

"Will you be around when I'm leaving, so we can have an official goodbye?" Xieny inquires.

"Yes, of course. I will do all I need to do now."

"See you both later."

"She's a good kid!" Lively grins when Xieny closes the door.

"Yeah, and she can cook too," Poet agrees, scarfing down the meal.

"Take it easy. You're eating as if someone wants to steal your food."

"I haven't eaten properly since Nhyira's been in jail."

"You up for a gift shop run? I want to surprise Xieny before she leaves."

"Any excuse to shop," Poet laughs, "I am all for it. Just let me finish this ice-cream."

Chapter 25

The moment Akio left the jailhouse Nhyira had an overwhelming feeling to pray for his safety. She grappled with it until she decided to be obedient. Placing a pillow on the ground she kneels and pours out her heart to God.

"Jesus, help me to find the words for this prayer. My heart is overwhelmed at the thought of something happening to Akio. Whatever it is that the enemy is trying, I rebuke it right now in Jesus' name. I pray that nothing will harm him. I speak against everything that tries to rise up against Your son. Guide and protect him. In Jesus' name I pray, Amen."

Trying not to become overwhelmed, she stares at the bland jailhouse food, opting not to eat it.

I hope that Akio brings me some diner food tonight.

Chapter 26

Akio hops out of his vehicle, surprised at the outline he sees in the diner. He marches into the restaurant.

Although he knew the menu like the back of his hand, he grabs one and sits in front of the man. "Care to explain why you're still in town, Zeki?"

"I don't have to answer you. My whereabouts isn't your business."

"I hope this has nothing to do with Nhyira."

"She's not the only person in town. Am I under arrest?"

"No."

"Then I don't have to speak to you. I just wanted a quiet meal. You're disturbing me."

"Zeki, if you know what's good for you, you'll leave town."

"That sounds like a threat, officer."

"I'm not joking," Akio snaps.

"Neither am I. My meal's ready. I'll be going now." Grabbing his take-out bag, Zeki nods to Akio. "Enjoy your meal."

Why is he by my jeep?

Running out of the diner, Akio approaches Zeki. "Why are you staring inside my vehicle? Did you put something in there?"

"I was checking out my reflection; didn't know this was yours," he mentions, while combing his hair.

"I can have you arrested."

"Relax man. I didn't touch your vehicle. I'm going."

Chapter 27

Yaniv strolls up from behind the jeep. "Hey man, what was that all about? Who was that?"

"A stalker if you ask me," Akio responds.

"He's stalking you?"

"He's stalking Nhyira. He's been visiting her in jail and parading himself around town as if they're friends."

"Can't you do anything about it?"

"He hasn't actually **done** anything, so legally I have no grounds to stand on."

"I would never understand how the justice system works," Yaniv counters.

"Let's talk in the diner," Akio replies.

"Things have been plateauing," Yaniv informs between gulps of his *Grapefruit Blitz*.

"Your company?"

"Between the newspaper articles and all the negative press from Canei's mother, sales have declined drastically. Some of my workers have quit. It's crazy."

"The business sector can be brutal at times," Akio adds.

"I've spoken to Canei's family, but they're not interested in hearing me out. The funeral was a huge mess and the family's bent on vengeance. It's like a witch hunt. They even started a campaign for Nhyira's trial to be pushed up."

"They're wasting their time. She's innocent and she will get out of jail."

"You really think so?" Yaniv raises his eyebrows. "I mean her aunt did spend 40 years in prison."

"What does that have to do with this case?"

"I don't think Celgagoas is as forgiving as they portray to be. One of the reasons that I have my headquarters elsewhere is because of how slow *Njapa* moves. Can you imagine a thriving business in *Zaire Valley?*"

"You're insulting the state you grew up in?"

"Not insulting, just an honest observation. Come on Akio, you work in *Kanomatton*. Admit it, *Zaire Valley* is backwards."

"You should stop while you're ahead. I work in *Kanomatton* because help was needed there."

"The opportunities were better," Yaniv corrects.

"*Njapa* is a quiet town and we like it that way. Very family oriented."

"Don't you **live** in *Kanomatton?* You have no defense."

"That's temporary."

Yaniv lowers his voice, "How's the investigation going?"

"We're using all the manpower we have to search all the databases. It's not as easy as TV shows," Akio counters.

"You guys need a technology **upgrade**. It's 2001."

Akio looks at his watch. "I have to go. Thanks for the talk. I'll let you know if I need anything else. I know we're close to solving this crime."

"I guess not as fast as you all would expect. Your girl's good and all, but the justice system here sucks. Hope you can catch the 'real' criminal," Yaniv jokes.

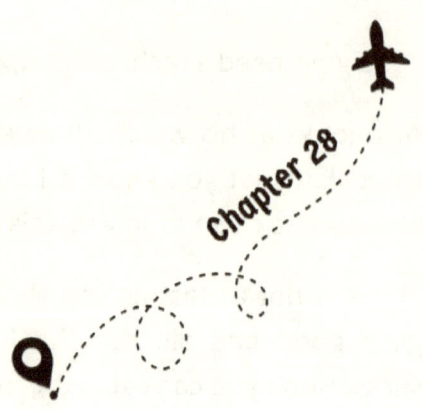

Chapter 28

Akio enters his vehicle and prays, "God, please intervene on this case. I know that You are a God of the impossible. My human senses want to agree with Yaniv that we have work to do in Celgagoas, but I know You don't operate on human logic. Please expose the true killer and free Nhyira."

He exhales and pulls out onto the road leading to the jailhouse. Driving into the intersection and seeing a car illegally speeding towards him, he tries to mash his brakes to allow the driver to pass, but instead crashes into a tree.

Mayleigh runs outside at the sound of the crash. "Someone call *75," she screams running towards Akio's overturned jeep. Sobbing uncontrollably, she tries to dial her husband's phone, but her fingers were numb.

Dear God, please let Akio be okay...

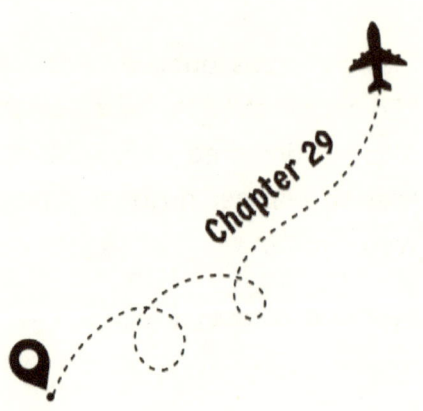

Chapter 29

Lively puts the final touches to the night's surprise dinner. Xieny's flight would be leaving in a few hours. She'd soon return from class to pack.

"You sure this surprise isn't lame?" Poet holds up a cupcake with a candle inside.

"Xieny's sentimental. She'd appreciate it. Shhhh. Shhhh. I think I hear her coming."

"SURPRISE!" the two women yell when Xieny enters the house.

"You shouldn't have," she grins happily. "Thank you Ms. Lively and Ms. Poet."

"Well, let's see it," Lively beams.

Xieny holds up her certificate. "I am officially registered in the **Starr Islands Wedding Bureau**."

"Why didn't I think of this before? You can help plan Nhyira's wedding... If she ever gets out," Poet finishes quietly.

"She will." Lively shoots her an encouraging look. "Tell us how the day went. Details. Details."

"Well, the judges loved my project. They said that it was the most original floral design they'd seen in a long time. I've been asked to return to *Njapa* to teach a class on event planning."

"Congratulations. I knew you had it in you. Of course, you know my house is always open."

"I sincerely appreciate all that you've done for me Ms. Lively. This house, the food, and company, surpassed expectations. I misjudged the citizens of *Njapa*," Xieny reveals.

"I'm glad that we were able to change your mind," Lively states looking at the certificate. "With all the bad press that we've had these past few years, it's a breath of fresh air to hear positive news."

"Have you decided on a name for your business?" Poet joins in.

"Not really," Xieny tilts her head. "I have some things left to take care of before I start. But, with this upcoming venture, my dreams may come true faster than expected."

Poet smiles, "I like seeing people focused on their goals. Determination is an excellent attribute."

"Yes, this year has been hard for my family, but I believe things will turn around soon."

The piercing ring of the phone startles the women.

"I wonder who that could be." Lively picks up on the fourth ring. "Hello. Lively here. Wait? Slow down. Slow down. What are you saying? Oh no. I will tell her."

Poet glances at her friend. "What's the matter?"

"Akio's been in an accident. That was Mayleigh; she's at the hospital with him."

"Is he alright?"

"She didn't say. We have to go meet her at the hospital."

Xieny looks at Lively with concern. "I'm sorry to hear about your friend. I wish I could've gone with you, but I have my flight tonight."

"I understand," Lively exhales, still shaking over the news. "We'll leave with you. I'm sorry that we had to cut your celebration short."

"No, no. You've done a lot for me. I'll get ready fast. Your friend's life is important. Thanks again." Xieny hurries to her room.

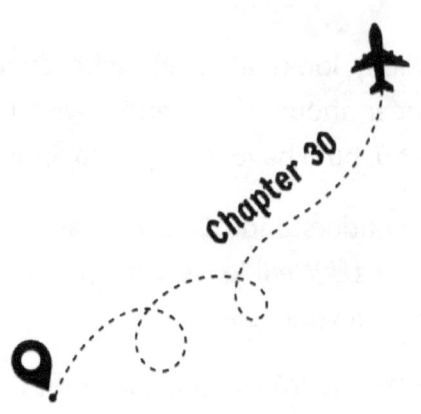

Chapter 30

"Mayleigh, why are you here this late?" Nhyira asks.

"I have some bad news."

She gasps. "Is it Aunt Poet? What happened to her?"

"It's Akio."

At the sound of his name, Nhyira's eyes widen. "Please don't tell me that—"

"He's been in an accident."

"WHAT?" she shrieks. "Where?"

"At the intersection outside the diner."

"When did this happen?"

"About 5 hours ago. I just came from the hospital. Your aunt and Lively are there now."

Nhyira begins to shake the cell bars furiously. "And I'm stuck in this stupid place. I should be there with him," her voice breaks.

"Don't worry sweetie, he knows you would be there if you could."

"NO! This isn't fair. He's always been there for me. **Always**. The one time he needs me, I can't be there for him," she sobs. "W-why is this happening, Mayleigh? Is this a sign that we shouldn't be together? First Akio moves, then my engagement to Jörn, then I end up in jail, now this? Is this the universe' way of saying that Akio and I aren't supposed to be together?"

"The **universe** is not in control, God is. HE will take care of everything. No need for you to worry."

"What happened? How did he get into an accident? Akio's not a careless driver."

"A speeding car."

"That doesn't sound right."

"Well, we wouldn't know full details until the police finish their investigation."

Nhyira rolls her eyes. "How long will that take?"

"I know, I know. But, Hesiquio and his team are doing everything they can."

"Is Akio okay?"

"Your man's a super soldier of sorts. Not a scratch on him. He insists his only priority is getting to you. Apparently, he was on his way here when the accident took place."

"This hurts my heart. He gets into an accident on his way to see me."

"These things happen. None of this is your fault. Cut yourself some slack."

"I wish I could cut these bars and get out of here."

"Look girl, I'm going to head home. Between the long day at work and those hours in the hospital, my body's shutting down. I'm no spring chicken and I have a baby to care for."

"Yes go. Thank you for coming. Take care of yourself. Drive safely **please**," Nhyira warns.

Staring at the wall, Nhyira exhales.

That's why I felt led to pray for Akio's safety. This is what Mayleigh meant by the Holy Spirit speaking to us.

Chapter 31

The next morning couldn't come fast enough; all Nhyira wanted to do was speak with her fiancé.

"I see you have your writing equipment out," Hesiquio notes.

"Apparently, my camera's forbidden in jail," Nhyira retorts, sarcastically.

"I know this is difficult for you. We're all working hard to get you out of here."

"Thanks Officer Zevallos."

"I got the results from the investigation."

Nhyira claps loudly. "That was fast. What did it say?"

"His brakes were cut."

"A deliberate attempt."

"That's what it looks like. We didn't see anyone on camera. Whoever did this monitored the cameras outside of the diner."

Nhyira's eyes widen. "Say that again."

"*Monitored the cameras?*"

"Oh my gosh, they're here."

"Um, who's here exactly?"

"The person who killed Canei."

"You think there's a connection?"

"**Don't you?**"

"We're still investigating—"

"My instincts are never wrong. Whoever did this was at the hotel and knows that I'm from *Njapa*. They also know that Akio is my fiancé." She strokes her chin.

"You look like you already have an idea who did this."

"There are only two people who fit that description."

Hesiquio pulls out a notepad. "I'm listening."

"I suggest you bring in Yaniv Vénissieux, the owner of *Royal Celgagoan Airlines*, for questioning. He was a classmate of Akio's and he has motive. His business could take a hit from all this negative publicity. Also, Zeki Montealpi, he was the bellhop at our hotel. Mayleigh made a comment about him possibly having a crush on me. He also came to visit me in jail. Both of them could have had access to the airhostess."

"I know Zeki; quiet guy."

"You know what they say about the **quiet ones**."

"We're not going off of speculations here, but I will bring them in for questioning. Do you have any other suspects?" Hesiquio asks.

"Shouldn't I be asking you that?"

"Let's be honest, between the limited technological equipment and the easygoing mentally of the *Njapa* police, you could've solved this crime if you were on the other end."

"Way to believe in your team, Hesiquio."

"I speak facts. We have to update our equipment and train our men to be thorough," he admits.

"This town hasn't experienced this much crime in decades, so it's fairly new. They're probably just accustomed to people running the red lights or parking violations."

"That's certainly changing."

"Maybe Ms. Higüey was on to something about *outsiders*."

"We're all outsiders, Nhyira. However, those crimes were committed by locals."

"That's the scary part," she shudders.

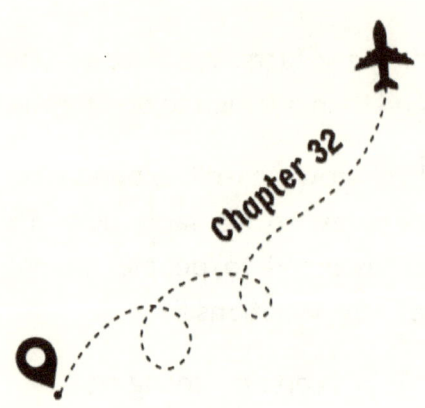

Chapter 32

Hesiquio escorts Zeki into an interrogation room.

"I didn't do anything," Zeki yells.

"Have a seat Mr. Montealpi."

"Come on Officer Zevallos. Why would I come here if I committed a crime?"

"I've seen all kinds of criminals over the years and have dealt with my share of narcissists and sociopaths."

"I'm neither of those. I'm a bellhop trying to make an honest living," Zeki continues.

"Yet, you've been to *Njapa* **twice** in less than a week? Doesn't sound like someone who's *trying to make a living* to me."

Zeki shrugs. "What can I say? I'm a saver."

"Where were you yesterday afternoon? Witnesses placed you at the diner. Akio stated that you had a confrontation and he found you near his jeep. You had enough time to cut his brakes and be on your way."

"After **Mr. Pretty Boy** told me where to go, I left. I went back to my hotel. I have several witnesses **there** that can vouch for me."

"You didn't leave the hotel at any point? It's not that far from the diner."

"Did you see me on the cameras?"

"I asked you a question," Hesiquio pounds the desk.

Zeki jumps. "I didn't leave the hotel. Sadly, I spent the rest of the afternoon **and** night watching movies."

Hesiquio scribbles some notes.

Zeki stretches his neck to see the pad. "What are you writing?"

"Official police business."

"If you're writing about me, it is my business. Am I being arrested?"

"No. But, don't leave town."

"Will you people make up your mind? You want me to go or stay? Which is it?"

"**Stay!**" Officer Zevallos snaps.

"OKAY! OKAY! Am I free to leave the station?"

"Yes."

"Send the next one in," Hesiquio calls out to another officer. He holds open the door for Yaniv to enter.

"Officer."

"Have a seat Mr. Vénissieux. Do you know why you're in here?"

"No. But my lawyer's on his way."

"It's only questions."

"Ask away." Yaniv sits up in the seat.

"Where were you yesterday afternoon?"

"You have to be more specific."

"Around 5:45," Officer Zevallos grumbles.

"I was on my way to my hotel in *Kanomatton*."

"There aren't any hotels in *Njapa*?"

"Not quite my style," Yaniv shrugs.

"What's the name of your hotel?"

"What's this all about? Am I in some sort of trouble?"

"Did you cut Akio's brakes?"

"What are you talking about? Something happened to Akio?"

"He's in the hospital; car accident. I'm sure you already know that."

"I had no idea," Yaniv looks stunned. "First I'm hearing about it."

"Akio said you two had a disagreement."

"Yeah, but he's my friend. I would never do anything to hurt him."

"What were you talking about?"

"Nhyira. Canei. This entire ordeal."

"And how is this *ordeal* affecting your business?" Officer Zevallos prods.

"I know how it looks, but I had nothing to do with any of this."

"We did an investigation ourselves and found out that you had ties to Canei."

"She worked for me."

"More than an employer-employee relationship," Hesiquio mumbles.

"Who told you that?"

"We're not as backwards as you think, Mr. Vénissieux."

"Oh, Akio told you," he chuckles. "You can call me Yaniv. Mr. Vénissieux's so formal."

"You find this funny? Tell me about your relationship with Ms. Zeriolor. Did she break up with you? Were you angry with her?"

"Our breakup was mutual."

"Well, she's not here to vouch for you, is she?"

"Don't even go there man. I would **never** hurt Canei. **Never.** If it's a suspect you're looking for, you have the wrong man. I wasn't even near that hotel. I have an airtight alibi. If I'm not being arrested, I'd like to be on my way. I have a company to run. I need to get back home."

Hesiquio cranes his neck. "You're not going anywhere until we get to the bottom of this."

"**What**? You have nothing to keep me here."

"You were at the scene of the crime, that's enough for us to arrest you. Make it easier on yourself and don't argue."

"I don't know what kind of bootleg police department this is," Yaniv scoffs, "but if anything happens to me you will be sorry. I will turn the entire *Njapa* police department upside down. That's why I left this stupid town in the first place." He throws over the chair, exiting the office.

Chapter 33

Akio sits up on his hospital bed and pops ice chips in his mouth. "How'd the interrogation go?"

"They're both pleading innocent," Hesiqiuo informs.

"No one wants to pay for their crime."

"Are you willing to press charges against them?"

"I don't see the point, Hesiquio. We don't have any proof that either of them did it. Besides, I'm fine. My car's banged up, but insurance will take care of that."

"You sure man?"

"I just want Nhyira out of jail. Did you find anything on the surveillance camera?"

"Whoever did it, timed the camera," Hesiqiuo continues. "This is no amateur. Yaniv would know about those types of technology with his airplanes."

"I don't believe he'd do something like that. What would be his motive?"

"He seems like a ruthless business man who only cares about himself."

"That's not the Yaniv I know. But one could never be sure."

"What about Zeki?"

Akio grits his teeth. "I don't trust him. Ever since the first time he came into town. How is he able to travel so frequently with his salary?"

"That's what I was thinking. Do you think he has connections in *Njapa*?"

"Nhyira. He's coming around like he's pursuing her. She's my fiancée not his. He needs to stay in his lane. Or better yet in his country. No man's going to follow a woman just to be a 'friend' to her. Whatever he wants, he won't be getting from her."

"She surely has plenty admirers," Hesiquio adds.

"Nhyira's an intelligent and beautiful woman, any man would want her. That Jörn character had better stay wherever he is as well." Akio's mind flashes back to Nhyira's previous fiancé.

"It's almost 2 weeks since she's been in jail. Nhyira helped get Mayleigh out of jail, so I'm working hard to get her out."

"Everyone's been working extra hard. However, I can't get over the fact that Nhyira would've solved it already."

Hesiquio throws his head back. "I said the same thing. She's extremely gifted. You'd better treat her right because she will find out."

"I have every intention of treating her like the queen she is. I love her. The doctor said that I should be able to get out before the day is over."

"You should stay and rest," Hesiquio advises.

"I feel great," Akio reveals. "All the lab results and x-rays came back negative. Nothing's going to keep me from visiting Nhyira today."

Chapter 34

"**Akio.** Akio. Akio. Akio. You're here. Awwww my *Occhisio*," Nhyira squeals, when he arrives hours later.

"*Mia Bella*. At least you're happy to see me." He pulls up a chair in the visitors' area. "How have you been?"

"Worried."

"About?"

"You obviously. I didn't get any sleep last night. When Mayleigh told me that you were in an accident, it broke my heart."

"I'm here now. You can't get rid of me that easily," he quips.

"I don't want to ever lose you."

"You won't." He strokes her face. "Is Olek coming in today?"

"He just left."

"Any progress?"

"Yes. He's at the lab working with a sound technician. Even though the cameras may not have picked up any visuals on the suspect, they're going to listen for unusual sounds. Background noises, etc."

"Good idea. Did you come up with that?"

"Nope. He did."

"He's getting better," Akio replies, impressed.

"I'm only his second client. Give him a chance."

"What are you thinking about?"

"Officer Zevallos told me that whoever cut your brakes monitored the surveillance cameras by the diner. That's exactly the same method used at the hotel."

"That's good. There's a pattern."

"I don't think the suspect will strike again though. Not when we're this close to solving the crime."

"I suspect Zeki."

"He didn't do it," Nhyira laments.

"Nhyira, I know you're a super sleuth, but I've been an officer longer than you've done this," Akio retorts.

"And?"

"Andddd... based on my **experience** some criminals play on their victims' emotions. You stated that you didn't see Zeki for the entire week you were at the hotel."

"I wasn't looking for him."

"But you have an eidetic memory and keen peripheral vision. Think. Did you see Zeki during your stay at the hotel?"

"Only that morning. He was surprised when we met."

"I find that hard to believe. You're popular in Starr Islands."

"Not everyone is up to date on current events," Nhyira replies. "Some people don't even know what's happening in their own neighborhood. So, it's highly likely that he is telling the truth. His body language was genuine. He hadn't seen me around."

"Okay, let's say he hadn't seen you prior—"

"He didn't."

"It doesn't mean he couldn't pin a murder on you. I mean he did have access to your luggage," Akio says.

"You're correct, but my bags passed through the original scanners in Amethyst Island with no trouble. Whoever did this accessed my bag from somewhere the baggage handlers work. That's the only way. Passengers don't have that much access to luggage, but airport personnel do."

"You're thinking Yaniv?"

"He has access, motive, and resources. I know he's your friend, but friendship hasn't stopped killers in the past. People who have a histrionic personality are great actors."

"It doesn't make any sense. This has messed up his business."

"Au contraire, if you look at it from another angle, it has also given him free publicity. Some people love publicity whether negative or positive. This crime has put his business in the headlines for almost 2 weeks."

"Do you really think Yaniv would go that far?"

Nhyira nods. "It's possible."

"He said he cared for Canei, why would he kill her?"

"Romance went sour. Jealousy. It doesn't take much. Maybe she knew something he didn't want getting out. And if she's anything like her mother, she was probably an outspoken woman and he wanted to shut her up."

"I don't believe this murder is about romance, it has to be that she knew something the killer didn't want getting out. Yaniv says that his sales have declined. Canei probably knew why."

"Exactly. Maybe Yaniv was taking from his own company. Some business owners do that."

"That's my friend you're talking about," Akio scoffs.

"Look at the past two murders I solved; they were both committed by *friends*. Let's take relationships

out of the equation. There's a killer on the loose
and they'll get caught…"

Detective Notes

Property of Nhyira Enosis

NHYIRA ENOSIS

DETECTIVE

MY NOTES

Yaniv Vénissieux. Ex-boyfriend of the deceased. (MY NUMBER ONE SUSPECT)

MOTIVE

- *Sour romance*
- *Canei had incriminating evidence against him?*
- *An argument that turned into an "accident".*
- *Felt pressure from her family to get back together. He didn't want her.*

Has the means to alter evidence (cameras, computer files, etc.). A private jet.

SUSPECT #2

~~Zeki Montculpi~~

MOTIVE

Liked Canei at the hotel. She rejected him?

CLUES

- *Stated that his business is declining.*
- *Shows up in Njapa after a long time away.*
- *Argued with Akio on the day of his accident.*
- *He has executive level access to both airports (Amethyst Island and Celgagoas).*

CLUES

- *Bellhop at the hotel.*
- *Tendency to fall for a woman easily.*
- *Showed up in Njapa just to visit me. TWICE!!*
- *Argued with Akio prior to his accident. He had enough time to commit the crime.*

NHYIRA ENOSIS

DETECTIVE

MY NOTES

Continued from previous page.

THOUGHTS

Even though Zeki is a suspect, I'm leaning more towards Yaniv. Based on his high level access at the airports. Maybe he was working with someone. He killed Canei, but had one of his workers switch my luggage. He would also have money to order a limited edition bag through overnight shipping. Or the "switch" could've taken place when I landed, while we waited for our bags. He ordered the bag after I left the hotel and then had it delivered in time for the switch.

ZEKI?

YANIV?

POSSIBLE TWIST IN THIS CASE

Yaniv and Zeki are <u>working</u> together. Yaniv committed the crime, paid Zeki to do the "ground work" cover up, find a "fall woman", and then said woman would be arrested upon arrival at the airport (that Yaniv has strong connections with).

FOLLOW UP

Ask Akio to find out if Yaniv and Zeki have any connections.

Ask Officer Zevallos to do a background check on Yaniv's personal bank account. Cross check to see if the money he lost in his business showed up in his personal account.

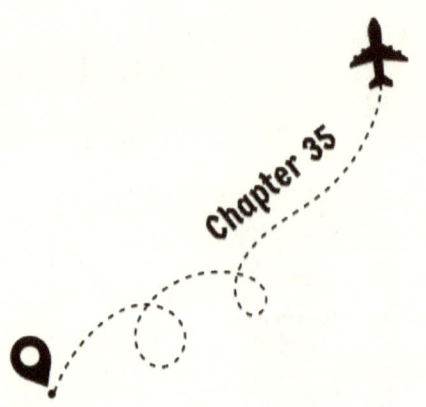

Chapter 35

The Next Morning

"Someone's at the door," Lively informs.

"Can you go see who it is please? My hands are deep in flour," Poet retorts.

Lively opens the front door, but sees no one. As she was about to close it, she notices a large envelope.

Poet comes into the foyer holding up her hands to prevent the flour from falling. "Who was it?"

"No one. It's just an envelope for you."

"Give me a minute; I'll go wash my hands to open it." She returns to the living room with paper towel to dry her hands.

Lively hands her friend the envelope. "It doesn't have a return address."

Inspecting it, Poet scrunches up her face. "This isn't even mail delivery time. Hmmmm."

"Well open it," Lively replies, inquisitively.

Poet begins to scream after she opens the envelope and reads its contents.

"What is it?"

"A practical joke. L-look at it."

The envelope contained a photograph of Canei Zeriolor's dead body in the closet and a note attached.

This picture is an exact replica of what will happen to all of Nhyira's loved ones if she doesn't mind her business. Too many prisoners because of her inquisitiveness.

"Who would do something like this?" Poet cries. "Haven't we already been through enough?"

"We have to take this to Nhyira," Lively suggests.

"That picture is too graphic. I don't want her to see it."

"This is Nhyira we're talking about. She isn't perturbed by gruesome images."

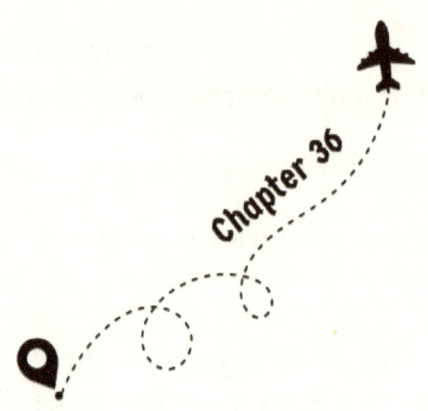

Chapter 36

"**Am** I in trouble again?" Nhyira inquires when she sees Poet.

Trembling, Poet hands the envelope to Nhyira. "You need to see this."

"Grab a chair from over there. It'll be 30 minutes before I'm able to come out from the cell for the day." Nhyira opens the envelope and observes the contents. After pausing, she smiles.

"Why are you smiling? This is a direct threat against you and all of us."

"Aunty Poet, I'm smiling because this is the break in the case I've been waiting for."

"I don't follow."

"Based on a discussion I had with Akio and this new development, I am now convinced that the killer has ties to someone in *Njapa*. Maybe not directly, but a relative of one of the men arrested. Note the words used, **"too many prisoners because of her inquisitiveness."** Only two men went to jail because of my investigation. The killer must be a relative of either Mr. Embleton or Abacus. The police have to investigate Yaniv or Zeki's relation to the prisoners."

"You're really calm about this."

"Can you bring this evidence to Mr. Pais and Officer Zevallos?"

"I will," Poet nods. "We'll be praying for you tonight at Mayleigh's house."

"I am grateful for your support. Thanks for everything Aunty."

"I should be thanking you. If you weren't *inquisitive*, I'd still be in prison. That's why I'm trusting God to bring you out."

Detective Notes

Property of Nhyira Enosis

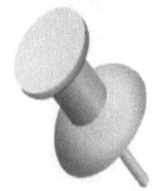

NHYIRA ENOSIS

DETECTIVE

MY NOTES

Yaniv Vénissieux. (<u>MY NUMBER ONE SUSPECT</u>)

NOTES

- *Related to Mr. Embleton? Previous worker? Cousin?*
- *Related to Abacus? Brother? Nephew? Cousin?*

THOUGHTS

- *The note was personally delivered.*
- *The killer is still in town/Celgagoas. Or frequents Celgagoas.*

SUSPECT #2

Zeki Montealpi

- *Related to Mr. Embleton? Nephew?*
- *Related to Abacus? Brother? Nephew? Cousin?*

FOLLOW UP

Ask Akio what's the update on the data from the list Yaniv gave him. Since Yaniv is a suspect, can we even trust his information?

LATEST TWIST IN CASE

- *Threat (note and photo) left at the mansion.*
- *No return address.*

✈

Hesiquio knocks on Nhyira's cell.

She looks up at him.

"They came back negative."

"Oh no, I thought the fingerprints found on the envelope would've helped."

"Sorry, but the envelope's clean," Hesiquio emphasizes.

"Our suspect is extremely thorough. Thanks for trying."

"Don't be discouraged, we're going to solve it."

"Can you do me a favor?" Nhyira asks.

"Anything."

"Keep the details about this investigation under wraps. Only those immediately involved with the case should discuss it. Mainly you, Akio, and Olek. Whatever details the investigative team already has, let them work with that. The killer is getting details from the news and if we're to solve it, we need to be quiet."

"That's a good point. I won't say anything else."

"Thanks," Nhyira smiles.

I know that I am missing something. Akio will be here this afternoon with the background check results. Jesus, please help me to think outside the box. Lead me to the right suspect...

Chapter 37

Akio drops the envelope on Nhyira's table. "I have the results."

"Took them long enough," she mocks.

"It wasn't easy to get background information for everyone, but the team worked around the clock to get it."

"I still don't understand why Yaniv would be forthcoming with this information."

"He didn't do anything," Akio pauses, "OR he's operating like a true criminal and wants to be *helpful* to throw us off."

"What do you think?"

"I don't think he did it; any of it. Also, he's not connected to Zeki. They're complete strangers."

"Did you run the background on Zeki and Yaniv's possible connection to Abacus or Mr. Embleton?" she inquires.

"I spoke to Hesiquio before coming in here and he says the database came up with no connection."

"I need some time to go over the documents."

"You want me out of here?"

"Please," Nhyira nods.

"Sure. I know you work best with no distractions."

"Thanks."

"I'll come back at 10PM," Akio adds.

Nhyira glances at his watch. "8 hours should be enough time."

"See you later *Mia Bella.*"

Nhyira spreads the papers all over the floor of her jail cell.

Promptly at 10, Akio raps on Nhyira's cell bars. "I'm back. I brought dinner from the diner."

"Thanks, but I'm not hungry. My eyes are burning."

"Are you finished with the files?" Akio asks.

"I am, but nothing's clicking."

"Talk to me."

"Zeki's only 'crime' is stalking. I don't think he has the means to commit something of this magnitude. And based on our conversations, he wouldn't be able to visit me without selling himself out. He'd have sung like a canary by now."

"What about Yaniv?"

"While Mr. Vénissieux may have all the resources to commit this crime and get away with it, I can't shake the feeling that we overlooked a key player. Though extremely subtle, it's highly plausible."

"I'm not following."

"What other member of the airline industry would have access to luggage? Maybe not directly, but they could've asked for help if they were friendly with the baggage personnel."

Akio looks puzzled. "I still don't understand."

"An **airhostess,** Akio. Think about it, Canei was an airhostess staying in the hotel. That means there would be other airhostesses staying with her."

"No other airhostesses were recorded in the files on the hotel's computers. It was just Canei."

"Airhostesses usually stay in the same location on their days off. One of Canei's coworkers would be familiar with her schedule."

"Yes," Akio's mind begins to work, "and that airhostess would have had access to Canei's room and could've 'slipped out' undetected because of the hotel's familiarity. That person would have known the layout of the hotel because they've been there before."

"Our killer could've locked Canei up and then committed the murder when they had their details finalized."

"Aka someone to take the fall," Akio finishes.

"And who better to take the fall than *Njapa's Crime Solver* herself? This person was at the hotel when we were there, maybe not for the entire week, but a few days. Have the tech team check for deleted files from the hotel's database."

"Your eyes are closing down."

"I'm exhausted," she yawns. "I don't want to miss anything."

"Go to sleep. I'll come back tomorrow," Akio suggests.

Chapter 38

The Next Morning

"You wouldn't believe what I found out," Nhyira beams.

"Did you sleep?" Akio asks.

"I couldn't. I was unscrambling all night. Our killer is clever; I have to give **her** that."

"Her?"

"Her," Nhyira nods.

"There were no women on our suspect list."

"I know and that's why it was the perfect crime. The suspect was here, well at least, around town for the entire time."

"What are you talking about?"

"Tell me the name of Lively's house guest again."

"House guest?"

"Yes."

"She came in for a class and has since left," Akio reveals.

"What I learned from solving my uncle's case, is not to rule out *'being out of town'*. I'm sure that you'll see her name on the airline's database. And she was in *Njapa* for 2 weeks. She was on the flight with me, not as an airhostess, but a regular passenger."

"You're serious about her as a suspect?"

"100%. It's the only logical explanation. Tell me her name."

"Xieny Fejős."

"Based on your background results only one woman was clever enough to do something like this. She's worked with the Royal Police Force in the past as a technology and linguistics specialist. But she's listed here as an airhostess of RCA," Nhyira divulges.

"Tech background, of course," Akio gasps.

"*Linguistics* is the key here. A mistress of words. I'm going to write some notes now and you'll tell me if it makes sense. I believe we've found our killer. I feel strongly about it. The team would have to conduct a thorough investigation, but I know I'm right." Nhyira hands Akio her notebook.

Detective Notes

Property of Nhyira Enosis

NHYIRA ENOSIS

DETECTIVE

MY NOTES

Suspect: Xieny Fejős. PSEUDONYM

NOTES	MOTIVE

NOTES

1. XIENY FEJOS

~~*JOSEFINE XY*~~

The name ~~JOSEFINE~~ is not listed in any of the documents.

2. SIEJE FONY X

- *SIEJE: Killer's first name*
- *FONY: A misspelling of phony*
- *X: As in X marks the spot*

There is a listing of a <u>SIEJE BOADA</u> in the air hostesses' list. She works for RCA, was listed on the schedule and on the same flight as Canei on the days leading up to the murder.

MOTIVE

Imprisonment for imprisonment. Her brother (Abacus) was sent to jail, so she wanted me to pay for it.

✈

"*Mia Bella*, you did it again. This is excellent. Come to think of it, I do remember Xieny passing by the diner the day of my accident. She could've cut my brakes then."

"Spending time with Aunty Poet and Ms. Higüey she would've gained insight on me and my whereabouts."

"And she probably paid someone to deliver the envelope at a certain time **after** she left town. I heard that she left town hours after my accident," Akio adds.

"You know what you have to do now?"

"Get you out of here."

Nhyira giggles. "Give the investigative team this evidence."

"My wife is an intellect. I am thankful."

"I'm not your wife yet."

"The moment you said yes to my proposal you became my wife," Akio winks. "When you get out of here, we **have** to celebrate your birthday."

"It's long overdue."

The Echo Journal

A SISTER'S REVENGE

February 22, 2001

What's done in the dark will always come to light. Two weeks ago we brought you the story of the murder of 26 year old Canei Zeriolor. In a fascinating plot twist only found in books, Nhyira Enosis has been acquitted of all charges.

Njapa's Crime Solver has done it again; this time from behind bars. After 2 weeks in jail, Nhyira has elucidated the true criminal.

Sieje Boada, an airhostess of the RCA and former coworker of Canei Zeriolor has been arrested for her murder.

After intense hours of searching and recovering of deleted surveillance files in both the Saseive Grande Hotel and the Royal Celgagoan Airlines' database, Sieje has been charged with first degree murder.

Open House!
Please contact
D. Sellers at
*88-01-20-4420
for more details.

A former member of the RPF's tech division, Sieje had been working with the RCA for 1 year. Her brother Abacus Boada was imprisoned last year.

Chapter 39

"Look at God." Mayleigh beams holding up a glass of *Passionfruit Blitz*. "Nhyira, if you don't become a PI then—"

"You know I'm not interested in that lifestyle," Nhyira finishes.

"We're going to pray about it because you'll make a great asset to this country's law enforcement team," Mayleigh adds.

"Okay," Nhyira shrugs. **"You** can pray. My heart isn't into returning to school. I'm just thankful to be a freed woman." She turns to Lively. "How are you feeling?"

"I can't believe I had a murderer in my house. She seemed so kind; did all the right things. Did she even go to class?"

"That's why I told you not to trust people you meet on the internet," Poet repeats.

"I am taking off my information from online. My house is no longer opened to the public," Lively mumbles.

Poet laughs and turns to Mayleigh with the tray of desserts.

"I have *Molten Table Macarons, Macadamia Cloud Torte, Teaberry Custard Ripples, and White Chocolate Peppermint Swivels* for everyone. Dig in," Mayleigh announces.

"You're trying to make me put on weight with all those sweets."

"You look good, Poet," Mayleigh encourages.

"It's time for us to leave." Akio takes Nhyira's hand.

"But, we're in the middle of a celebration."

"Girl," Poet scoffs, "you better go with your man. You've celebrated with us enough."

Chapter 40

Taking off the blindfold, Akio leads Nhyira to an aircraft.

"Hold up, hold up. How are you able to pay for this?"

"I know you have your own money, but I told you I'll take care of you. I don't want you to worry about anything."

"This is a private jet, Akio."

"Yaniv has gifted me the jet for the night. I wanted to celebrate your birthday in style."

"I don't think I could apologize enough for accusing him of being a murderer."

"He's forgiven you, but he still wants to be in your next book," Akio chuckles.

"I know just the character for him," Nhyira snickers.

Akio brushes a strand of hair from her face. "I don't know what you're doing, but keep it up. You look *gawjus*."

"I so want to correct your spelling. Why'd you do that to me?"

They sit down in the aircraft dining area. "You know I'm playing with you," Akio flirts.

"Drinks, sir?" the waiter asks.

"Sure. Pour for the lady first."

"Happy birthday Ms. Nhyira," the waiter says.

"How'd he know my name?" she asks, when he was out of ear shot.

"Tonight's all about you *Mia Bella*."

The waiter returns with a tray of food. "Your meal courtesy of Mr. Qvareli."

"You cooked this?" Nhyira stares at Akio, stunned. "Since when do you cook?"

"I took lessons. Your aunt and Mayleigh have been teaching me for a few months. I wanted it to be a surprise."

"You mean to say you could've cooked all this time and we were eating out?" Nhyira giggles.

Akio winks at Nhyira. "I wanted your birthday to be extra special."

Taking a bite of the meal, Nhyira begins to choke.

"Nhyira, what's wrong?"

"Nah, I'm just playing. It tastes so good."

"You better not do that again," Akio exhales, relieved.

"I'm thankful. I'm alive, free, and celebrating my birthday with the man I love. What more can I ask for?"